DEBBIE AN
HER NAP

by Dr. Frances R. Horwich

and Reinald Werrenrath, Jr.

Illustrations by   Adele Wehr

RAND McNALLY & COMPANY • Chicago

Why DEBBIE AND HER NAP was written . . .

This story was written to help young children enjoy getting ready for their naps, and to help them accept the idea of a nap as a regular part of their day's activity.

I hope your child and Debbie become good friends.

Miss Frances

THIS is a story about a little girl named Debbie.

One bright, sunny day Debbie played
outdoors most of the morning. She played
in the backyard with her tricycle and her
wagon. She had some boards and boxes,

too. She did many different things with them.
   She rode her tricycle back and forth on the narrow sidewalk, pretending she was a policeman checking the cars.

She filled the wagon with twigs and leaves,
and pretended to deliver them to a man who
wanted them for his yard.

With the boards and boxes she built a zoo. Then she jumped from cage to cage, pretending she was a monkey, then a lion, and last a kangaroo.

Playing with all of these things was a lot
of fun, and Debbie had a very good time.
The morning went so fast that she was sur-
prised when her mother opened the kitchen

door and called, "Debbie, it's lunchtime!"
Debbie took time to put her tricycle and
her wagon in the garage. Then she hurried
into the house through the kitchen door.

Her rubbers were wet and muddy from playing in the grass. She took them off near the door. Then she hung her overalls and her sweater in the clothes closet.

Debbie looked very happy. She felt very happy. Her cheeks were red. Her eyes were shining. Her hair was mussed from her cap.

She ran into the bathroom and washed her hands. Then she went to the kitchen where her mother was waiting for her.

They sat down to lunch. Debbie told her mother some of the interesting things she had done during the morning. How she had played policeman on her tricycle. How her wagon had been a delivery truck. Her mother laughed when she heard that Debbie had been a monkey, a lion, and a kangaroo.

Debbie ate every bite of her lunch, and asked for a second glass of milk, because she was really hungry.

After lunch her mother invited her to help clear the table and wipe the dishes. This pleased Debbie, because she liked to help her mother in the kitchen. She carried each dish very carefully from the table to the sink.

When the table had been cleared, her mother gave her a dish towel. Debbie wiped each dish dry and then put it on the table. When all the dishes were dry, her mother put them in the cupboard.

The last dish was on the cupboard shelf
when her mother said, "Debbie, do you know
what time it is?"

Debbie looked up and smiled. Then she whispered in her mother's ear, "Yes, it is nap-time."

Her mother laughed. "That's right. Let's go."

Together they went to the bedroom. Debbie sat down on the rug and took off her shoes. Next, off came one sock—then the other. Up she jumped. Her mother unbut-

toned Debbie's dress and pulled it up over her head. Where was Debbie? Her head was caught somewhere inside. Gently her mother reached inside the dress and loosened the collar, which was caught on Debbie's ears. Then she pulled the dress the rest of the way, and out came Debbie!

While Debbie took off her slip, shirt, and panties, her mother got Debbie's pajamas down from the hook in her closet.

Debbie yawned and smiled. She was tired because she had been playing outdoors in the air and sun all morning.

Into her pajamas climbed Debbie.

While she ran to the bathroom her mother took off the bedspread. She folded it carefully and put it on Debbie's chair. Then she fluffed the pillow and pulled back the blanket and sheet.

Here came Debbie with her hands clean.
"Smell my hands," she said.
"Mmm—soap," said her mother.

Debbie climbed into bed.

Up came the sheet, then the blanket. Her mother bent over and kissed Debbie gently on the forehead. "Have a good nap," she said.

"I will," Debbie sang.

Her mother tiptoed quietly to the window
and opened it softly. She pulled down the

shade and walked to the door. She turned
around to smile at Debbie.

Do you know that Debbie did not see her mother smile? She was already asleep.

Her mother closed the door very gently and said to herself, "Debbie will have a fine nap because she had such a happy morning."